For my family
Britta Teckentrup

First American edition published in 2007
by Boxer Books Limited.

Distributed in the United States and Canada
by Sterling Publishing Co., Inc.
387 Park Avenue South, New York, NY 10016-8810.

First published in Great Britain in 2007
by Boxer Books Limited.
www.boxerbooks.com

ISBN 13: 978-1-905417-50-6
ISBN 10: 1-905417-50-0

1 3 5 7 9 10 8 6 4 2

Printed in China

HOW BIG IS THE WORLD?

BRITTA TECKENTRUP

Boxer Books

One morning Little Mole woke up
with a big question for papa.
"How big is the world?" asked Little Mole.

"Why don't you go and find out?" replied papa.
So Little Mole popped out of his little molehill
in the middle of a big field.

"How big is the world?" asked Little Mole
when he met a tiny spider.

"As big as my web,"
the spider replied.
"My web is the world.
There isn't any more."
And the spider crawled away
to the end of her world.

Little Mole came upon a mouse.
"How big is the world?" he asked.

"As big as my field," replied the mouse.
"My field is the world."
And the mouse scampered away
to the end of his world.

"How big is the world?" Little Mole asked a horse.

"I happen to know that it is bigger than this field,"
replied the horse, as if he knew all about the world.
"The world goes all the way to the sea. That is the end
of the world," continued the horse.
Then he trotted away.

"How big is the world?" Little Mole asked a seagull.

"As big as the ocean, I think," the seagull replied.

"What is the ocean?" asked Little Mole.

"It's all that water splashing about,"
said the seagull.

"Come, I'll show you."

They flew out over the ocean.
Little Mole watched the world grow bigger and bigger.

"What's that?" called Little Mole,
shouting over the wind.
"A whale," replied the seagull.
"Can we go and say hello?" asked Little Mole.
"Hold on tight then," said the seagull.

"How big is the world?" asked Little Mole.
"MASSIVE!" replied the enormous whale.
"Jump on and I'll show you."

They traveled north to where the ocean
was so cold it had turned to ice.
"Is the whole world so cold?"
asked Little Mole, shivering.
"I know warmer places," replied the whale.
And the whale turned and swam south.

The ocean was calm.
The air was warm.
And as the sun went down,
the sky became red.

"Where does the world end?"
asked Little Mole.
"End?" replied the enormous
whale. "I have swum in this
ocean all my life, and
I have never seen the end."

Soon, moonlight danced on the waves.
"The world is beautiful, isn't it?"
said Little Mole.
"The more you look,"
replied the enormous whale,
"the more you will see."

They saw a **vast** desert ...

a **tall** city ...

huge mountains ...

wild jungles ...

colorful creatures ...

and thick forests.

"I miss my family," said Little Mole.
"Then it is time to take you home,"
said the enormous whale.

"Are we there yet?" asked Little Mole.
"Nearly," said the enormous whale.
"Look, Little Mole, there's the seagull."
Little Mole thanked the enormous whale,
and the seagull flew Little Mole all the way home.

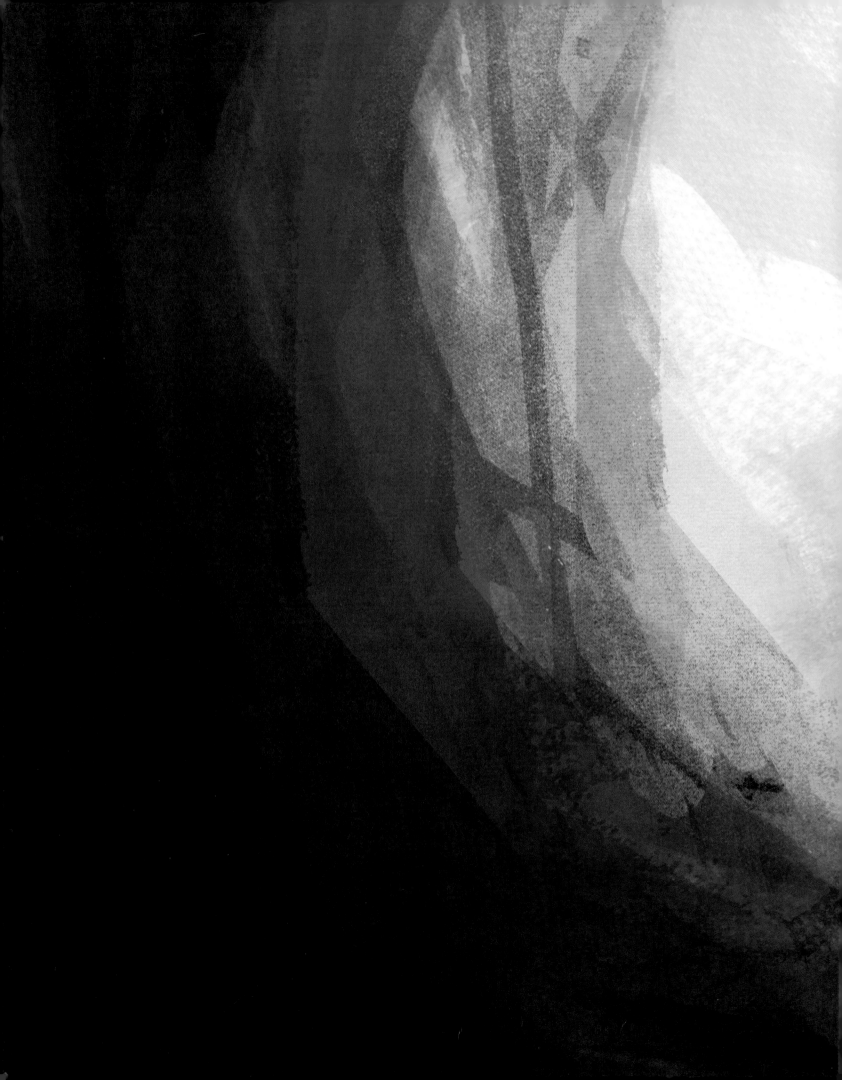

Little Mole popped down into his little molehill.

It was very late, and very quiet.

Everyone was asleep—except papa.

"How big is the world?"
whispered papa.
"As big as you want it to be,"
said Little Mole quietly,
and he went to sleep.